THIS CANDLEWICK BOOK BELONGS TO:

_____

_____

_____

_____

For Billie
S.G.

For Les and Nell
C.S.

First U.S. paperback edition 1996

Library of Congress Card Number TK

ISBN 1-56402-599-3

2 4 6 8 10 9 7 5 3 1

Printed in Hong Kong

This book was typeset in New Baskerville Educational.
The pictures were done in watercolor and ink.

Candlewick Press
2067 Massachusetts Avenue
Cambridge, Massachusetts 02140

FOUR BLACK
PUPPIES

Sally Grindley
illustrated by Clive Scruton

CANDLEWICK PRESS
CAMBRIDGE, MASSACHUSETTS

Four black puppies in a basket

fast asleep.

One black puppy waking up.

One black puppy

going for a walk.

One black puppy

pulling on an apron.

One shopping baske

falling down.

CRA

Three black puppies running

n to take a look.

Three black puppies seeing . . .

A GHOST!

One white puppy

chasing three black puppies.

All four puppies running

around and around.

All four puppies

running back to bed.

All four puppies in a basket

fast asleep.

SALLY GRINDLEY received a degree in French literature before working in children's book publishing. Now the mother of a young child, she plays tennis, gardens, and writes children's books.

CLIVE SCRUTON holds degrees in graphic design and illustration. After working in advertising and cartooning, he turned to children's books in 1980 and has since illustrated twenty-three picture books.